The Special One

The Story of a Police Dog

WRITTEN BY TRISH KEATING ❧ ILLUSTRATED BY BILL TIERNEY

This story is dedicated to all Canine officers and their partners.

EDITED BY BEV GAUSE ❧ DESIGNED BY ALAN WELECZKI

ISBN 1-886991-00-6

PRINTED BY GOPHER STATE LITHO, MINNEAPOLIS, MINNESOTA

shamrock
Publishing, Inc. of St. Paul

On a cool May night while the city of St. Paul slept, a litter of German Shepherd puppies was born. Their mother cleaned and nursed them in the comfort of their warm bed.

As the puppies grew, their owner could see that one was more curious, more courageous and more playful than the others. From morning until night this puppy was on the go, exploring and discovering new and interesting things.

At night, while his brothers and sisters slept, he would guard the house to keep his family safe. The owner called this puppy The Special One.

As time passed, The Special One grew into a beautiful dog. His brothers and sisters were given away to neighbors and friends, but the owner kept him, knowing he had a special purpose in life. The question was, what would that special purpose be?

One day while reading the newspaper, the owner came upon an ad. It read
WANTED: GERMAN SHEPHERD DOGS FOR THE ST. PAUL POLICE CANINE UNIT
CALL OFFICER JIM LONG AT: 555-0276

"That's it!" exclaimed the owner. "A police dog!" He knew then that he must give The Special One this chance. He called the Canine Unit and spoke to Officer Long, the head dog trainer.

Officer Long said, "We would love to come and see your dog. I will send an officer out tomorrow."

The next day a member of the St. Paul Canine Unit came to the owner's home. The Special One barked loudly as he greeted the officer with excitement.

"How are you doing, fella?" the officer asked while patting him on the head.

The officer tested The Special One to find out if he had the natural qualities needed to make a good police dog. First, he checked his sensitivity to noise. The Special One wasn't afraid when the officer slammed his clipboard on the step.

Next came a test of his play drive and energy level. "Let's see how you like playing fetch," said the officer. The Special One chased after the ball until he caught it. After each catch he brought it back, eagerly waiting for the officer to throw it again.

"What do you think?" the owner asked. "Does he have what it takes to be a police dog?"

"He does appear to be a good candidate for the Canine Unit, but I would like to take him to the training center for more testing," the officer replied.

The owner then signed a paper allowing The Special One to go to the Canine Training Center.

The owner felt sad when his dog rode away in the squad car, but he knew now his Special One had a chance to be a valuable member of the police department. That made him feel better. Waving good-bye, he shouted, "Good luck, boy!"

The Special One liked riding in the squad car.

He barked to the people he passed on the streets.

When the car pulled into the Canine Training Center, The Special One could hear other dogs barking from inside the building. The officer helped him out of the car.

"Good boy," he said as he led The Special One to his kennel.

After a short time, Officer Long came to get The Special One for more tests. He tested his intelligence, confidence and courage. Officer Long also tested The Special One's noise sensitivity and play drive once again. The Special One passed all the tests with high scores and was given treats for his good behavior. Officer Long could see that The Special One was indeed a good candidate for the Canine Unit.

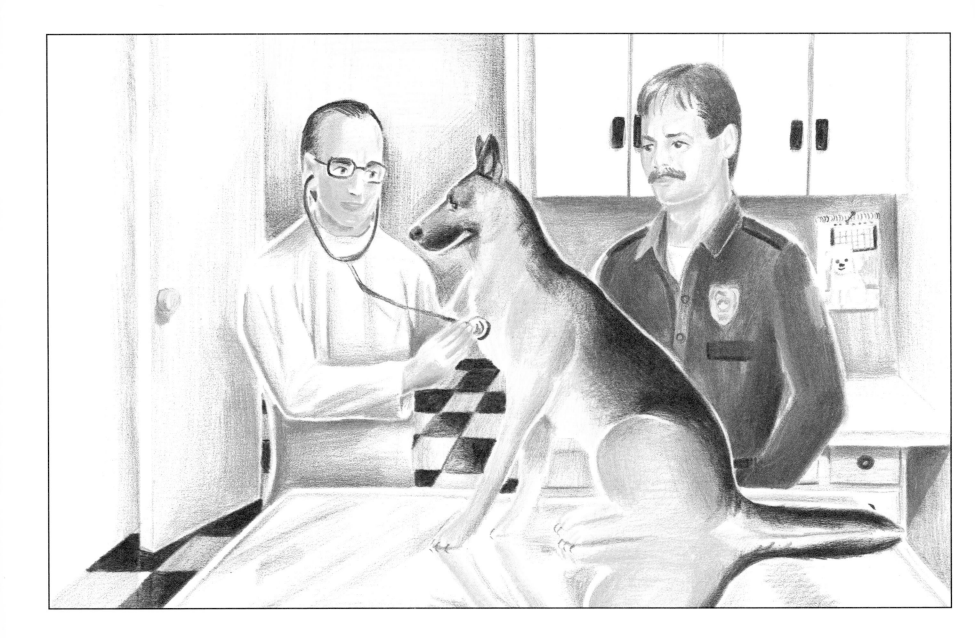

The next day another officer took The Special One to the veterinary clinic. There, The Special One was given a medical exam to check his health and an x-ray to see if his hips were strong. After his exam, the doctor told the officer, "This dog is in excellent health. His hips are good and strong and should be able to withstand the athletic life of a police dog."

16

When The Special One had passed all his tests, it was time to be assigned to an officer who would be his partner and handler. The head trainer knew that his best officer needed a partner. This officer was very brave and strong and always worked very hard. He needed a dog that was also brave, strong, and hard-working.

Officer Long believed that The Special One and this officer would make a perfect team and assigned them as partners.

Max was such a smart dog that it wasn't long before he learned his new name and became a loyal member of the officer's family.

Max spent hours playing in the backyard with the children.

The officer had to give his partner a name. The name he chose was Max.

He opened the kennel gate and said, "Max, come." Then he took Max home to meet his family.

Always he guarded their home, making sure they were safe.

Sometimes he would go for long walks through the woods with his family.

Other times they would play in the park by the pond.

After a few months, Max and his partner began their training. Every day for fourteen weeks, they went to school at the Canine Training Center near St. Paul.

First, Max and the other dogs would be groomed by their handlers. Max liked it when the officer brushed his coat until it was shiny.

After the dogs were groomed, they would line up outside with their partners. Officer Long would inspect them, making sure they looked their best for work.

Exercise was the next step in getting Max and the other dogs ready for police work. Police dogs must be in good physical condition. They work very hard and must not tire too fast.

Max's partner would exercise him by going for long walks through the woods.

Sometimes they would run, jumping over large rocks, darting in and out of trees and bushes. Max loved running and playing with his partner.

Other times they would work out on the training field. The field had an obstacle course that Max and the other dogs had to learn. There were ladders to climb, a window to jump through, a tall platform to walk across, a long box to crawl through, and hurdles that looked like different kinds of fences to jump over.

Max was nervous the first time he climbed the ladder to reach the top of the platform. He had never done this before and wasn't used to being so high above the ground. He felt better when his partner said, "That a boy, Max. You're all right."

24

The officer also used the exercise time to teach Max obedience and good behavior. All police dogs must be on their best behavior when on duty.

He would say, "Max, stay!" and Max learned to stay. He would say, "Max, come!" and Max learned to come. The officer always rewarded Max for his good behavior. "Good boy," he would say while hugging him and patting his back.

Before long, Max knew all his commands and was able to run the obstacle course without making any mistakes. He especially liked jumping over the hurdles and through the window. When he was done, his partner was always there, waiting to reward him with praise and affection.

Max grew to love the officer as his master and friend.

Like all police dogs, Max was taught to find people and objects using his sense of smell. He learned to recognize a human scent.

For practice, one of the other officers would hide in one of six large wooden boxes on the training field. When his partner gave the command, "Find him!" Max would sniff each box until he found the human scent. Barking loudly, he would announce he had found the person hiding in the box.

Max was also taught how to react to gunfire. He learned that when he heard gunshots, the situation was very dangerous. He knew he must protect his partner by attacking the source of the gunfire.

The last thing Max learned was how to stop someone who tried to run away from a crime scene or threatened his partner. Max loved and respected his partner and would do anything to protect him.

When the officer gave the command, "Get him!" Max learned to chase a suspect until he was caught. Max would take hold of his arm and not let go until his partner would say, "Max, leave!"

After Max learned all he needed to know to be a police dog,
he graduated from the Canine Training course and
was certified by the United States Police Canine Association.

Max and the officer were a dedicated police team
and loyal friends. Together, they had one of the best criminal
apprehension records for the St. Paul Police Department.

Their courage and dedication to the people of St. Paul
will long be remembered.

With Special Thanks

Officer Jim Long	Norm and Florence Knaak	Alan Hendrickson
Officer Brad Jacobsen	Gail Knutson	Larry Bangert
Officer Dan Murphy		Chris DeNet
Officer Mark Ficcadenti	Liberty State Bank	Jane Lecy
Officer Jon Sherwood	O'Gara's	Jeff Harrison
Officer Pat Lyttle	St. Paul Pioneer Press	Dan O'Gara

A note from the author

From its conception, The Special One's purpose was to educate children as well as adults about canine officers and their partners. I hope you have gained that knowledge.

However, I also hope you could sense there was more to this book than just words accompanied by beautiful illustrations. This book is about family, friends, co-workers, teachers and acquaintances who demonstrated incredible amounts of enthusiasm and support for the project. It is about canine officers who recognized its educational value and willingly offered their assistance. It is about giving something back to all who have given.

For me, The Special One is and will always be more than a book. It is a gift given to all who contributed and believed.

Thank you,

Trish